P9-DOC-489

An I Can Read Book™

This 2010 edition was created exclusively for Sandy Creek
by arrangement with HarperCollins Publishers.

Sandy Creek
122 Fifth Avenue
New York, NY 10011

ISBN 978-1-4351-2648-0
Manufactured in China
Manufactured 04/2010
10 11 12 13 14 15 SCP 10 9 8 7 6 5 4 3 2 1

flowers

pony

garden

present

kite

recipe

lemons

sand castle

photo

scrapbook

ponies

table

A Secret Gift

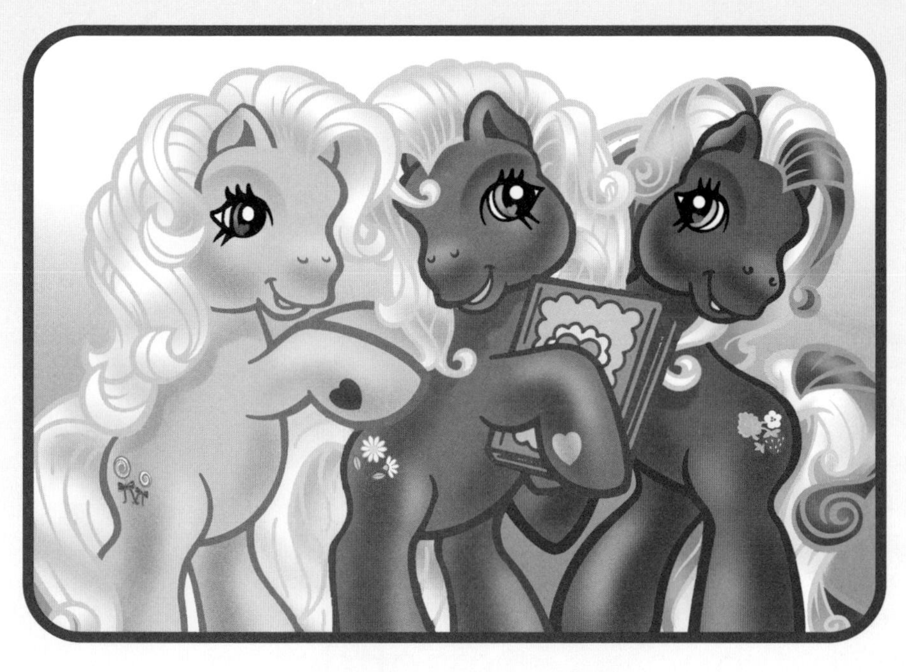

by Ruth Benjamin

illustrated by Gayle Middleton

Daisy Jo was a happy .

She loved working

in her .

She loved the smell

of her .

Most of all, she loved

doing nice things

for her  friends.

Butterscotch wanted to thank

Daisy Jo for being

such a great  friend.

"I will make a !"

said Butterscotch.

"The other  can add

to the .

When it is finished, we will

surprise Daisy Jo with it!"

Butterscotch called a meeting

in the Café.

The  liked the idea!

"I will add a  to the  ,"

said Fluttershy.

"This  of Daisy Jo

and me making a

at the beach is perfect."

GLUE

"I will add dried 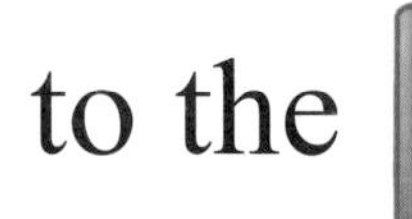

to the ,"

said Star Swirl.

"Daisy Jo and I both

love .

Daisies are her favorite,

of course!"

CRAYON
CRAYON

"I will add Daisy Jo's

favorite cupcake 

to the ,"

said Sweetberry.

"Daisy Jo likes cupcakes with

 and chocolate chips.

Yummy!"

1 dash
of
PLUS
2
of
FLOUR

Just then, Daisy Jo walked in.

She saw the  hard at work.

"What are you doing?" she asked.

Butterscotch hid the 

under the .

"It is a surprise!" said Butterscotch.

"Meet us tonight at the Café

to find out what it is."

"A surprise," said Daisy Jo

to herself.

"My birthday is soon. . . .

Are the  making me an

early birthday  ?"

she wondered out loud.

"What could it be?

Maybe a  ?

Or a poem?"

HAPPY BIR

Back at her house,

Butterscotch looked at the  .

She added a drawing

of Daisy Jo in her  .

"This  is filled

with good memories.

Daisy Jo will love it!"

Butterscotch said.

That night, the  met

at the Café.

When Daisy Jo walked through

the door, the  shouted,

"Surprise!"

"We made this  for you,

Daisy Jo," said Butterscotch.

"We wanted to thank you for

being such a great  friend."

"Wow!" said Daisy Jo.

"I tried to guess what the

surprise would be!"

Daisy Jo was happy.

The [ponies] were the greatest

friends she could ever ask for.

"Thank *you* for being

such wonderful 

friends," Daisy Jo said.

"I love my  .

It is the best surprise ever!"

by Ruth Benjamin

illustrated by Ken Edwards

balloons

brush

butterflies

cake

castle

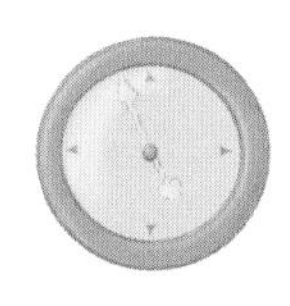
clock

crown

kite

necklace

ponies

pony

prize

ribbons

star

wind

The [pony picture] were excited

about the Best Friends' Ball.

Twinkle Twirl was busy

at the dance studio.

Sweetberry was busy

baking a [cake picture].

Bakery

At the ,

the worked hard.

They blew up .

They tied the

with shiny .

Welcom
to
Best Frie

Skywishes left the .

She stopped to visit

Twinkle Twirl.

"Do you want to fly a

with me?" asked Skywishes.

"I can't now,"

said Twinkle Twirl.

"I am teaching the

a new dance."

WELCOM

"I will leave the  here.

Twinkle Twirl might

play with it later,"

said Skywishes.

Inside, Twinkle Twirl

looked at the .

"It is time to get ready,

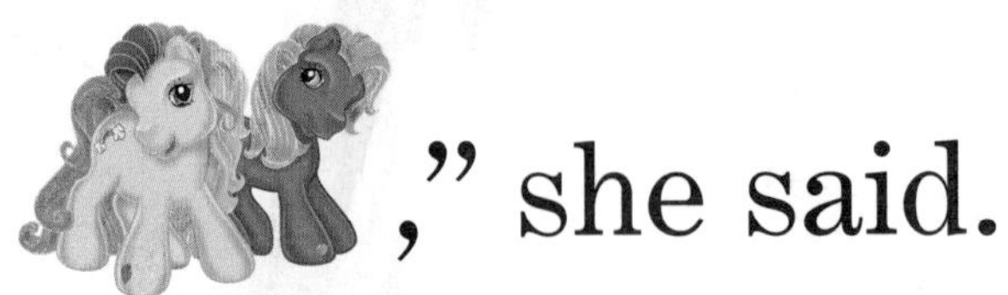," she said.

Dance Studio

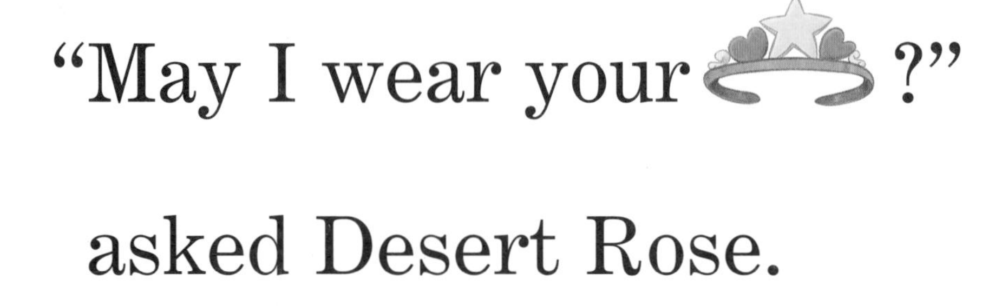

"May I wear your ?"

asked Desert Rose.

"Do you have a for me?"

asked Applejack.

"Will you my hair?"

asked Starbeam.

"Of course!" said

Twinkle Twirl.

"I love to help my friends!"

It was time for

Twinkle Twirl to get ready.

She had no .

She had no .

She had no one to 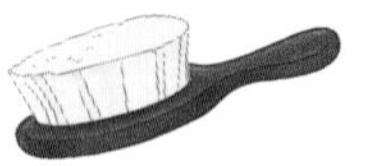

her hair.

How could she go

to the ball?

You're Invited
to the
Best Friends'
Ball!

Twinkle Twirl looked up

at the .

Skywishes'  was

flying in the .

"A wishing star!" she said.

"I wish I had a 

and a .

Then I could go to the ball."

"Your wishes *will* come true,"

said a pretty .

 were all around him.

"My name is Catcher."

"Wow!" said Twinkle Twirl.

"You are a real

pegasus ."

 Catcher and her magic  placed a  on Twinkle Twirl's head. They gave her a new . Twinkle Twirl was ready for the ball!

You're Invited
to the
Best Friends'
Ball!

Twinkle Twirl went

to the .

The were

happy to see her.

"Thank you for being

kind and helpful.

You are the best friend

ever!" they cheered.

She got a special .

Twinkle Twirl was

the ★ of the ball.

But the best part of all was

being with good friends–

best friends forever!

Caps in the Air!

by Karen Sherman
illustrated by Lyn Fletcher

 breeze

 cap

 caps

 diploma

 gown

 ponies

 school

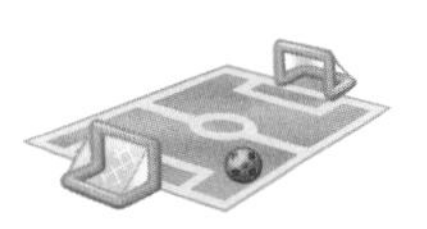 soccer field

 sun

 tassel

 tassels

 theater

Graduation day was here!

Rainbow Dash was very happy.

She put on her pretty .

She put on her pretty .

She shook her head.

Her  twirled.

It was time to go!

The  skipped

through Ponyville.

The  was shining.

The  was blowing.

Their 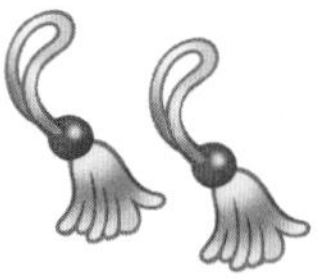 twirled.

Then Rainbow Dash said,

"My  is gone!"

The  looked up.

They saw the 

in the air.

It flew like a kite.

The was like a tail.

The blew away.

“Oh, no!” said Rainbow Dash.

“What will I do

without my  ?”

“Don’t cry!”

Scootaloo said.

“We are your friends.

We will help you find it!”

First, the looked

in the .

"Remember when I was too

shy to sing?" said StarSong.

"You made me brave!"

Rainbow Dash smiled.

But her

was not there.

Next, the  looked

on the .

"Remember when we lost

a big game?" said Scootaloo.

"You cheered me up!"

Rainbow Dash smiled.

But her was not there.

Ponies 0 1
Visitors 0 2

The  went to look

in Cheerilee's beauty shop.

It was closed for graduation.

"Graduation!"

said Rainbow Dash.

"We'll have to hurry.

I'll go without my ."

CLOSED

The  ran

to the  .

They were just in time.

Rainbow Dash

went up on the stage.

She got her  .

"Well done, !"

said Cheerilee.

"We are graduates!

We worked hard.

And we worked together.

It's time to throw

our in the air!"

P

All the  cheered.

They tossed their 

high in the air.

The  twirled.

"Are you sad?" asked StarSong.

"We did not find your ."

"No," said Rainbow Dash.

"I am a graduate!"

Rainbow Dash said.

"I worked hard.

I do not have a .

But I do have my friends!"

Ponies on Ice

by Ruth Benjamin
illustrated by Carlo Lo Raso

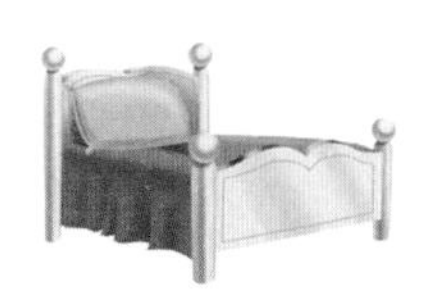
bed

crowns

feathers

gift

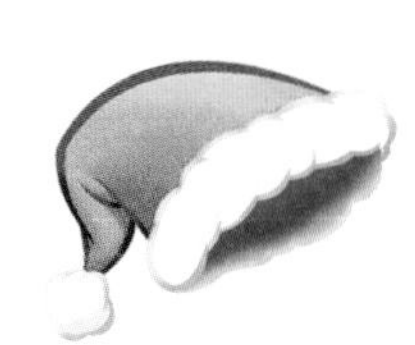
hat

ice skates

icicles

necklace

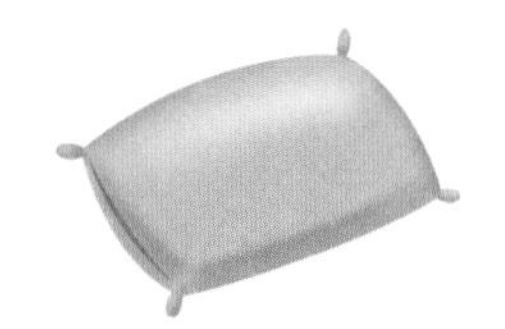
pillow

pond

ponies

pony

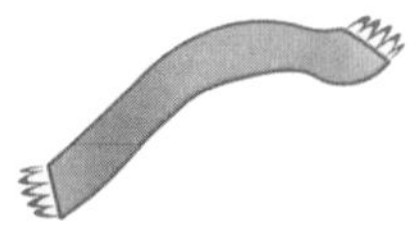
scarf

sun

trees

It was winter in Ponyville.

 hung from the .

The was frozen.

The were getting

ready for the ice-skating

party.

Each was planning

an ice dance for the party.

Triple Treat tied her  .

Then she worked on flips.

Bumbleberry tied her 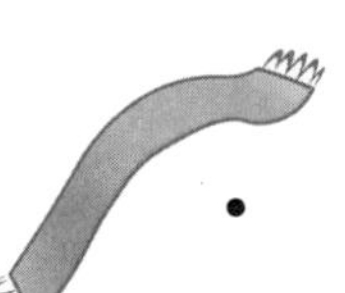 .

Then she worked on twirls.

Kimono put on her  .

Then she tried figure eights.

Pinkie Pie watched

the other  skate.

She could not do a flip.

She could not do a twirl

or a figure eight.

What would she do

on the  ?

Triple Treat saw Pinkie Pie

sitting by the  .

Pinkie Pie looked sad.

“What is wrong?”

asked Triple Treat.

“I do not know any tricks,”

said Pinkie Pie.

"I will teach you tricks!"

said Triple Treat.

"Follow me!"

Pinkie Pie tied her .

The two went out

on the ice together.

Triple Treat showed

Pinkie Pie how to spin.

She showed her

how to skate backward.

She showed her how to jump.

Pinkie Pie saw the

around Triple Treat's neck.

"This is my lucky  ,"

said Triple Treat.

"I want you to have it."

"Thank you!" said Pinkie Pie.

"I will wear it tomorrow

when I skate on the  ."

That night as Pinkie Pie

got into,

she thought about the party.

She wanted to show the 

what she had learned.

She put the  under her.

She dreamed of 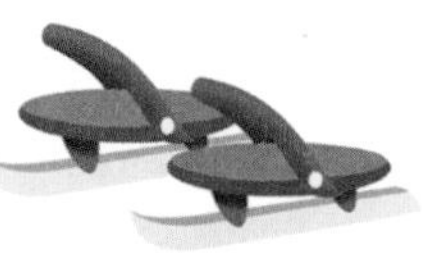.

The next day, the  shone.

It was a good day to skate!

The  were dressed

in fancy costumes.

The costumes had sparkles,

, and .

Pinkie Pie wore the .

It was time for Triple Treat
to skate.
She asked Pinkie Pie
to join her.
They skated backward.
They did spins and jumps.
The lucky  sparkled.

"You are the star of the day!"

the  cheered.

"Thank you!" said Pinkie Pie.

And she showed them

a fun new trick.

Sleepover Surprise

by Ruth Benjamin
illustrated by Josie Yee and Carlo LoRaso

 birds

 books

 card

clock

 cookies

 door

 eyes

 flowers

hot chocolate

 house

 mailbox

 pajamas

 ponies

 pony

 ribbons

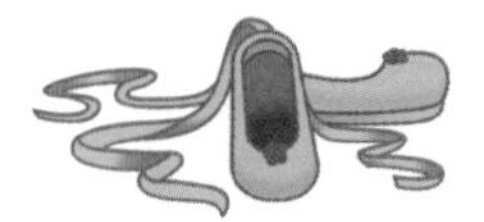 shoes

 sun

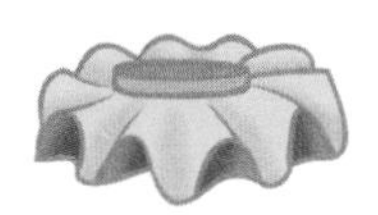 tutu

Inside every  in

Ponyville was a 

from Cherry Blossom.

She was having a

 party!

All of the 

were invited.

The invite read:

Please come to my  *party*

tonight at midnight!

We will have 

and .

Bring your favorite

 *to share.*

Be sure to take a nap

so you are not too sleepy!

Love, Cherry Blossom

Petal Blossom was

the first  to get ready.

She loved parties!

She put   in her hair.

She put on her .

She took a nap.

Triple Treat made 

for the party.

She put on her  .

She took a nap.

Star Swirl picked 

to bring to the party.

She tied the 

with ribbon.

She put on her .

She took a nap.

Skywishes wished

she could take a nap.

But she was not tired.

She put on her dance

 and her 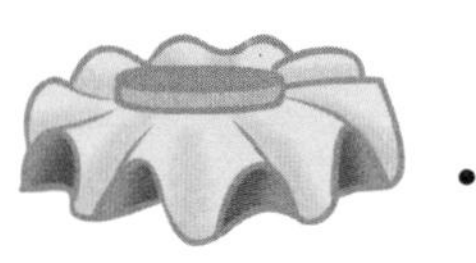.

She danced until

the  went down.

Back at home, Skywishes

put on her .

"I am sleepy from dancing

so much," she said.

She looked at the .

"It is almost time

for the party.

I will close my

for just a minute."

At midnight,

the  went

to Cherry Blossom's  .

They drank 

.

They ate  .

They read  .

"Where is Skywishes?"

they wondered.

The next morning,

Skywishes woke up.

The was shining.

The were singing.

She looked at the  .

"Oh, no!" she cried.

"I missed the party!"

12 1 2 3 4 5 6 7 8 9 10 11

Skywishes heard a

knock at the 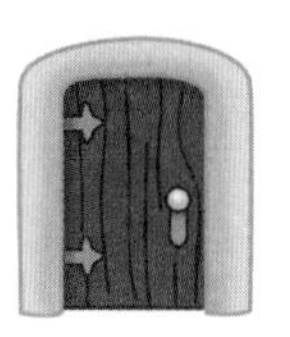 .

It was Cherry Blossom

and the other  .

"I am sorry I missed the party,"

Skywishes told them.

"We missed you!" said

the  .

"So we brought the party to you!"

“Skywishes smiled.

“You are the best friends a pony could ask for!” she said.

Tutus and Toe Shoes

by Ruth Benjamin
illustrated by Lyn Fletcher

 barre

 bottles

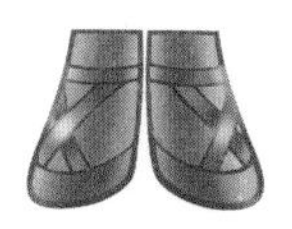 feet

 flowers

 hairbrush

 piano

 ponies

 pony

 ribbons

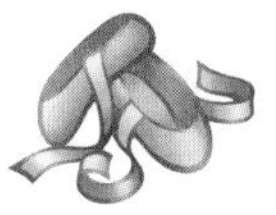 toe shoes

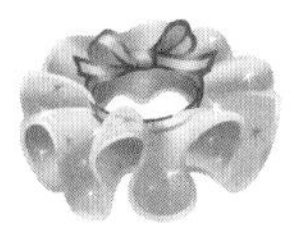 tutu

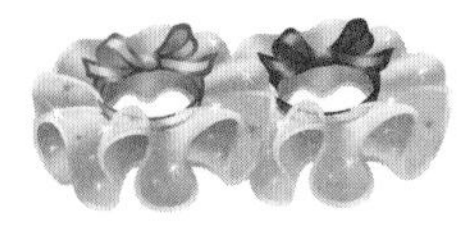 tutus

Twinkle Twirl's dance school

was about to open.

She had everything ready.

The  waited outside.

"Welcome to  dance

school!" called Twinkle Twirl.

Twinkle Twirl's
School of
DANCE

First, Twinkle Twirl taught

the how to dress.

"Ballerinas wear a 

and , and

in their hair.

You should pack a dance

bag with your clothes,

, and your ."

Twinkle Twirl told the 

to bring  of water.

"Dancing is hard work!"

she told them.

"Spinning in your 

will make you thirsty!"

Next, Twinkle Twirl taught

the  the five positions.

They stretched at the 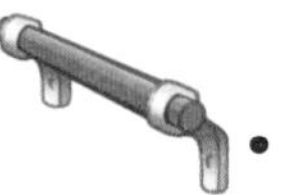.

They pointed their toes.

They waved their arms.

They bent to touch

their .

Soon it was time

for the  to dance.

Two by two,

they moved across the floor.

They held hands

and skipped their 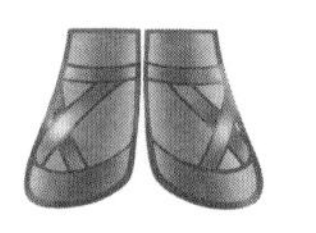 .

Their bounced

and their twirled.

Twinkle Twirl showed the

 how to leap.

She showed them how

to be light on their 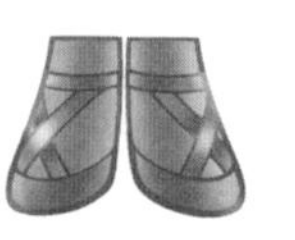 .

Her flew with her.

"Now each will try

a leap," said Twinkle Twirl.

Pinkie Pie was afraid

to leap across the floor.

She hid behind the  .

Then she tripped

on her laces.

Oops! She fell to the floor.

"What happened?" said Cheerilee.

"I was scared to try a leap," said Pinkie Pie.

"Sometimes teamwork can help!" said Rainbow Dash.

Pinkie Pie fixed her  .

She was ready to try.

The showed

Pinkie Pie what to do.

“Bend your knees and lift

your arms,” said Cheerilee.

“Now point your 

and jump!” said Scootaloo.

“You can do it!” they said.

Pinkie Pie leaped.

The  cheered.

"Hooray!" said Twinkle Twirl.

Rainbow Dash gave

Pinkie Pie .

"I could not have done it

without you," said Pinkie Pie.

"Friends are the best part

of dance school!"

Pinkie Pie took a bow.

"I can't wait to come back!"

she said.

Very Lucky Ponies

by Ruth Benjamin
illustrated by Lyn Fletcher

 bag

 book

 butterflies

 butterfly

 clouds

 clover

 cupboard

 grass

 pie

 ponies

 rainbow

 scooter

 sugar

 sun

 sunflowers

 wind

It was a rainy day.

The [clouds] were dark.

Serendipity saw

something in the [grass].

It was shiny and green.

It was a four-leaf [clover].

She picked up the [clover].

Suddenly the rain stopped.

The  came out.

The dark  went away.

A  sparkled

in the sky.

"Wow!" said Serendipity.

"I think this

is a lucky  ."

At home, Serendipity

found her missing .

"I have looked all over

for this !" she said.

"This  really is lucky."

Serendipity wanted

to share the 

with the .

Tidy Up!
Princess

She gave the 🍀

to Desert Rose.

“Now you will have

good luck, too,” she said.

“Thank you,” said Desert Rose.

“I will bring the 🍀

when I go to pick flowers.”

Desert Rose found a field

filled with pretty .

She had never seen

 before.

“This  really is lucky,”

she said.

Then she gave the 

to Scootaloo.

Scootaloo rode her 

to look for .

She saw a 

with a pattern.

She had never seen

"This really is lucky,"

she said.

Cupcake was baking a .

Oh, no! She ran out of .

Scootaloo came by and gave

the to Cupcake.

Cupcake checked the 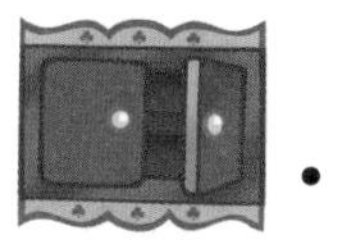.

She saw a big  of .

"This really is lucky,"

she said.

SUGAR

Cupcake wished

all the 

could have a lucky .

Just as she made her wish,

a big gust of  came.

The  blew away.

"Oh, no!" called the .

Our lucky is gone!"

The looked all over

for the .

But they did not find it.

"We should not be sad,"

Desert Rose told the  .

"We do not need the 

to feel lucky.

We are lucky that

we have each other.

We are good friends!"

"Yes, we are!"

said the .

"We are very lucky !"

Then they shared a 

under a !

Winter Festival

by Ruth Benjamin
illustrated by Lyn Fletcher

dragon

footprints

hill

icicles

map

pond

ponies

snowball

snowballs

snowflake

snowflakes

sun

unicorns

wind

Winter had arrived!

There was snow

on the ground.

There were  on the trees.

The  were getting ready

for the Winter Festival!

They were excited to welcome

the  to Ponyville!

The  built an igloo.

They made 

for the toss.

They baked cupcakes

topped with 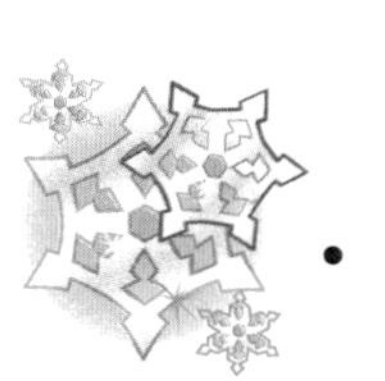 .

They baked cookies

with snow-white chips.

The next day,

when the  rose,

the  were ready

for the Winter Festival.

But the  were not there!

"Where are all the  ?"

asked Scootaloo.

!FESTIVAL!

"I will look for the ,"

said Minty.

"What if they got lost?"

"I will help you,"

said Spike the .

"We can use my 

to find the way!"

“Check the ice garden,”

said Spike.

He read the .

At the garden, they found

lots of  and snow.

But they did not

see any  .

"Look!" cried Minty.

"Here are  in the snow!"

Spike and Minty followed

the to a big snowbank.

The  were behind it!

"We found you!" said Spike.

"Did you forget about

the festival?"

"We remembered,"

said Rarity.

"We were on our way.

But we saw a pretty 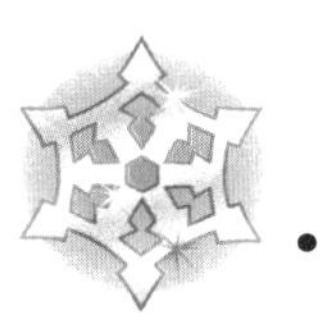.

It was the prettiest 

we had ever seen.

We watched the 

dance in the ."

Ponyville

"We followed the 

up a ," said Rarity.

"Soon we were off the path

and trapped here!

We couldn't see the way back.

We are so lucky you

found us!"

"We are so glad you

are safe!" said Minty.

"My will lead us back

to Ponyville," said Spike.

"Great!" said all the  .

"We promise not to run

after any more !"

All the cheered

when they saw the  .

"Now the fun can begin!"

said Minty.

Spike built snow  .

Scootaloo made snow angels.

Rarity skated on the 

.

Soon the began to set.

"This was the best

Winter Festival ever!"

said Rarity.